Guilty and Innocent

BY

Donna Sako

COPY WRITE & DISCLAIMER

This is a work of fiction, Names, characters, Business, places, events, and incidents are either the products of the author's imagination or used in a fictitious manner. Any resemblance to actual person, living or dead, or actual events is purely coincidental.

ISBN 978-0-9906794-6-2

DEDICATION

This work is dedicated to Book Chat and Writer's Circle members for their support and dedication.

Table of Contents

Chapter One: The Beginning

It was dark. The moon was full and glowed creating shadows resembling those created in daylight with the sun. Cicadas sounding their voices were heard among the silence while lightening bugs added sparkle within the trees and brush. A large shadow began to emerge and roam the woods. It began walking slowly, pausing on occasion then walking once again. The brush was heard moving as the shadow continued to make its way toward a cabin in the distance. It was then I realized the shadow was me. But what was I doing in the forest?

Slowly I moved closer to the cabin entrance and began to open the door. It creaked slowly as it opened. I was curious but afraid. The cabin was empty. A fireplace was seen across the room. As I slowly entered my footsteps echoed. Why was I here?

A wolf's howl began. It was getter louder. The wolf was coming. I quickly closed the door and grabbed an abandoned chair the came into view from behind the door. Placing the chair against the door, I braced for the possible attack to come.

I screamed and suddenly awoke. It was a dream. But what did it mean? The overhead fan was rotating providing a slight breeze. Was this a warning? I have had dreams before and they have predicted events but what the event is...this is unclear.

Reliving the dream I began to look for clues. Although the cabin was scary, it did provide me with some protection from the wolf. So perhaps I need to look for protection? The protection might seem scary but the wolf is scarier.

But what was I doing in the woods? Did I have a choice? Or was this the environmental condition? Dark with some light but not glowing? True the virus was spreading but now it is there but thanks to vaccines it was slowly getting under control. There were some flickering lights from the stars and lightening bugs which could represent things are getting better. The mostly quiet night, however, had cicada's sounds. Those sounds could be the constant noise from the news which was calming but noisy at the same time.

I was walking in the woods. Was the woods the earth? My country? Or my community? It could be all. But what is this wolf howling in the distance but moving closer to me? I need to listen closer. There was a move "the Wolf of Wall Street". Could another Wall Street of corruption be coming?

I have been reading recently of day traders using their bets to raise prices on stocks and lure people falsely into buying them and later selling their stocks when the price goes up causing others to lose. If this is done on a grand scale a crash could occur.

Recently Bitcoin has been fluctuating but rising. If there is nothing to back it but new people but not any real value other than betting, that could hurt, especially since the banks are now investing in bitcoin. The dangers are there. I have to act.

But what do I do? Where is this cabin? Could it be gold? But what if gold also loses its power? After all gold, once again, is only based on the faith of everyone believing in it.

Chapter Two: The Job

The alarm rang and it was time for me to ready for work. Rushing about brushing teeth, washing face and dressing during which I was still pondering my dream.

Once I reached work I took a moment to view the sky. The sun was shining but there were threats of storms later in the day. Climate change is real. This has been a year of storms, disease, riots, corruption, fires, floods, and economic stress. Much like the seven plagues of Egypt in the Bible. But who needs to be set free to end these?

One of my biggest faults is trying to solve ALL the things I see. I am a detective but working for the FBI allows me to see things others do not.

"Good morning Mary"

Smiling as I entered the room I replied, "Good morning to you Dan as well. How are you feeling today? Yesterday's raid was a bit intense."

Dan smiled, "Yes, it was but as usual we got through it. Our boss, Steve Williams, wants us to look at another case. We are to be briefed soon."

"Thanks for the heads up. I am going to grab a coffee."

The room was filled with agents busy talking, typing, and walking about looking at files or just drinking their coffee. Much like a normal day at the office.

Mary got her coffee and sat at her desk turning on her computer checking her email.

A loud voice was heard through speaker. "Briefing in 15." It was the boss, Williams. Everyone gathered their notepads, coffee and pens and walked to the end of hall into a mini theatre where they sat in small desks with cup holders attached. There was a mini stage with a podium where speakers could easily view the staff. A microphone was attached to the podium. Bantering was heard as they waited for the boss.

Williams soon walked in loaded with paperwork accompanied with his secretary who sat in small desk nearby.

"Good morning everyone." The room became quiet. "Recently we have been tasked with a case that will require your talents." He looked around the room and smiled. "You may have heard recently about some small crimes that have been occurring. Some are email scams. Others are thefts and recently a murder." Everyone was listening intently. "We think these are related. Fingerprints and other normal traits seem to missing. Whomever it is, they are well trained and have kept below our radar. But it is this hiding that is so well done that seems to connect them." Everyone was looking at one another. "This person or persons may be a professional. So I need all of you to review the cases and look for ANY other connections so we nab them. The cases will be delivered to your desks within the next hour. Some you will need to partner, especially the murder case. But all results and updates will be shared with everyone. Thank you for your time."

As Williams closed his notes and he and his secretary left the room, light conversation was heard throughout.

"Mary, what do you think?" asked Dan.

"I think I would like to work on the murder case."

"Me too!"

16

Chapter Three: Investigation Begins

A haze was lingering over the hillside. The sky was full of clouds which darkened the day. Dark skies, rain, and weird weather seems to have become the norm. Things were changing.

"Mary?" asked Dan, "are you okay?"

Dan was hovering over Mary at her desk with a concerned look upon is face. Mary was staring out the window and then suddenly seemed to awake from a dream.

"Dan, sorry. I was just thinking about how the weather has changed recently." Mary looked over at Dan. "I'm okay, just being a bit thoughtful."

"Well, thought I'd just tell you. We did not get the murder case. They gave us the stolen car which was found outside of town off the road after it had a minor crash." Mary just looked at Dan with no expression. "Mary, are you awake?" Dan snapped his fingers and then waved his hand in front of her eyes.

Mary smiled and began to laugh, "Of course I am awake! So what does the case say about the crash?"

"Thank goodness, glad your back." Dan laid the case on the table and sat next to Mary. "According to the file, the car was stolen from Ohio and driven to Maryland. There were no prints even the owners when found. Because it was wrecked, the owners collected the insurance and left it to us. Us being the FBI to find the thief or thieves. They still have the vehicle in storage. It is due for destruction soon so...I thought we might go and examine it. What do you think?"

"Okay. Perhaps we can see where it was abandoned as well."

They copied the file and then grabbed their jackets leaving the original file locked in their desk.

They reached the storage area and began to examine the car. It was not a fancy one. It was an old 2000 model Ford sedan. The front of the car was dented from the crash. As they looked though it Dan found some candy wrappers. "Not sure, but they might find some DNA on these."

For the most part there was no clue that even explained why the vehicle was stolen other than for transportation.

"Okay, we need to check the crash site." Dan nodded in response.

They drove to a remote highway near a forest and parked their car. "Mary, what are we looking for?" Dan asked.

"Dan, I just have a feeling that we might find a clue here."

As they left their car, Mary was looking at the side of the rode and found strangely enough some tire tracks embedded in some deep mud. They followed the tracks and found the tree where the car was abandoned. "I can't believe the tracks are still here. It has been at least two years. Mary, I think this happened right before you came to our unit."

Mary, opened and looked in the file. "You're right. It was right before I arrived."

They searched but still found no more clues. "How does this vehicle link to the other cases?" Mary asked.

"No clue. I guess we will need to wait for the update from the other cases at our next group meeting."

"Could the murder be linked to the driver of this car?"

"Guess that is what the lead detective thinks."

As they drove back to the office, Mary was reading the file. "Dan, the car dent was not very strong. So they were not driving very fast. Did the car have gas in it? I need to call the storage area." Mary quickly dialed them and they quickly answered. "Hello, this Mary Fife, DOI, we were there and viewed the Ford 2000 sedan earlier. Was the gas tank empty when it arrived?" She waited as they checked. "Why was that not in the report?" Again she was listening. "Thanks, when is the car due for destruction? And where are the materials found by you inside the car?" Again she waited. "Thanks, you've been quite helpful."

Dan glanced at Mary as he drove, "Well? What is it?"

"No, gas. So the car was pushed or slowly driven into the bush to hide it. Because no blood was found or other incriminating evidence no foot prints were even looked for since the car was reported stolen after it was taken about one week later."

"Seems it was reported rather late. Reason why?"

"At first the towing company thought the owner just ran out of gas and they had to wait until their contacts for tracing the owner could tell them the owner's phone number. The vehicle registration showed the name but the ID only showed the insurance company and their claims office was closed, also there was no idea how many days had passed since the car was put there. Because the owner's never reported it missing until it was found, it was assumed they knew the driver. The only reason the car was not destroyed earlier was because of the back log due to the pandemic. The owner of the vehicle came and took their materials before the police could get there. So no links were found. The towing company who picked up the car, washed the car inside and out after the owner left after picking up their materials at the instruction of the owner. The reason given was they planned to sell the car as is and would be in touch. They never called so the towing company reported it to the police and it made its way to us"

"So the owner knew or was the driver?" Dan asked as he drove.

"It seems. But the owner has seemed to vanish. The car ID was not real and the insurance company was given fake information by owner as well. While they had the car, they paid the insurance and gave contact information but the car ID was not real because the owners were non-existent. That is according to the file. So the owner was very good at hiding everything. "

Dan's eyes were wide open in surprise. "Mary, I guess our boss is right. This person or persons are pros. What about the phone?"

"It turned out to be a burner phone."

"So the question is, what was the car used for as well as by whom?" Dan shook his head. "Okay. So what was the name on the ID?" Mary began to laughing quite hard. "Mary what is no finny? Mary what is the name?"

Dan began laughing hard as well as he heard the name. "John Doe!"

Chapter Four: Filtered

The briefing room was slowly filling up as Mary and Dan were sitting waiting for the meeting to begin. Only three days had passed since their excursion. But they were interested in what others had found. Perhaps the stories would somehow begin to blend.

Steve Williams entered, sat in his chair and patiently waited for everyone to arrive. Soon the room was full and became quiet as he arose and came to the speaking post. "Attention everyone." The speaker made a bit of an echo at first, but once adjusted, his voice became clear. "Thanks to all of you for your examinations and reports. After reviewing the results we were able to clear several of the unsolved cases and now have only a few left. Of those left we plan to see if there is a link between them and the murder case. "

"Ours should be included" Mary whispered to Dan.

"Murder occurred in a remote area near where a stolen car was found. Thanks to the team of Dan Jones and Mary Fife, we believe, the cases may be connected. There was also a robbery near that area about the same time in which the victim may have some connection. The robbery case was investigated by Pat Reed and John Dye for whom we also give our thanks. These 3 cases will be combined and assigned to these four agents who will work with me going forward."

"Yes!" whispered Dan as he looked for the other agents in the room.

"I wish to thank all of you for your closing of the many other cases which had been delayed due to our staff challenges these past two years. Other than the four working with me, the rest of you may be dismissed. New cases will be assigned as they arrive. Once again thank you all!"

After a few minutes the room was clear except for Mary, Dan, Pat, John and their boss Steve Williams who was waving them come toward him. "Please come forward." They rose and moved closer. "Here is a copy for each of you of the cases." Steve said as he passed them folders," I want each of you to review each case individually and then we will meet in two days to discuss."

"Could be meet with each of our normal team members beforehand? It is just that we find talking to one another helps us solve cases." Mary asked.

"Sure I see no problem but please read the files in full before you discuss them. If you want to each team can communicate as well if that helps. No action on the cases until we meet in two days." He said as he left the room.

"Thank you sir." Mary responded before he closed the door.

Pat smiled and whispered, "I am glad you mentioned we can discuss with one another. I work with John the same way."

John and Dan were also smiling and shaking hands as they had a brief conversation.

Mary smiled as she responded to Pat, "You're welcome. I thought you two worked like us as well."

"Well I guess I need to read the files. See you later!" John said as he left the room followed by Pat.

"Mary thanks for the mention of discussing it with our team. I guess we'd better get reading as well!" Dan smiled and they also left to read the files at their desks.

Chapter Five: Invisible

Mary chose to read the murder file first. The murder took place in a cabin in woods in western Maryland not far from where the car was abandoned. The man was decapitated with a hatchet and found in his bed. He was renting the cabin for a fishing trip and seemed to be alone. Perhaps he rented it alone but invited a friend or was invaded by the car abandoner.

Then she read the robbery which occurred in a small town about two miles away. It was a gas station with a hardware store inside and was robbed while closed when but gas purchases were still allowed with credit cards. No evidence of gas purchased. The hardware store was robbed of tools and one of them was a hatchet. The store also logged fishing supplies and other survival items as well as some quick food. So she could see a possible connection.

If the murder was committed using the stores hatchet, then it must have occurred after the robbery. That is unless the murderer robbed it afterwards as build-up to their cover-up. So timing between the two events not in conclusive.

The body was not found by the cabin owner for three weeks. The owner delayed cashing the check given for the month rent and when he finally cashed the check it bounced. So he went to the cabin to confront the renter.

Interesting enough, the check was signed by John Smith another generic name which it turned out to be a fake checking account. The checks were bought on line via a business who would print checks based on information given. The service was paid for with

PayPal account established by John Smith as well. Money was deposited via a cash process which was untraceable.

So the victim seemed to be unknown until they did a DNA test and found he was actually from Ohio and his name was Henry Ford! What were the odds! Could he have been the John Doe who stole the car? If so, who murdered him? But the car was stolen and abandoned over a month from the murder. How did Henry get to Maryland? He had no car at the cabin. Could he have been driven here by John Doe? But the cabin was not rented until a month after the car was found. Where did John Doe and Henry Ford have stayed until the cabin? Especially if the car was abandoned.

These events seemed to be connected but it is sure a bizarre story for sure.

Chapter Six: Sharing

Dan read the cases as well and was looking forward to a discussion with Mary. He called her and made an arrangement to meet her for lunch.

It was beautiful day. The sun was shining through the windows of the restaurant which was a bit blinding for Dan as he waited patiently for Mary. Soon she drove up and exited her car. Dan watched as she locked her vehicle but dropped the keys soon after. Mary seemed a bit frustrated as she picked up her keys from the ground and placed them in her purse.

Mary entered the door and began looking for Dan. He was waving from a booth near the back. She began to laugh as she moved toward him. "Just what is so funny?" Dan asked.

"It is just that you looked so cute as you waved." She chuckled as she sat across from him in the booth. "So how did you like the information we were given?"

"Well, good afternoon to you as well. Can't we just enjoy our meal a bit before we get to work?"

"Sorry. Good afternoon. It is just a habit. Sure we can wait." Mary smiled. "So what is on the menu?"

They spent the next few minutes discussing the meal choices. The waitress came over to their booth. "Good afternoon. What can I serve you today?"

"I would just like a burger and fries with a large coffee black." Dan replied.

"And you?" asked the waitress looking at Mary.

"I think I would like a grilled cheese with small side salad."

"Great! And what would you like to drink?"

"I would like hot tea, Earl Grey, if you have it."

"Yes, we do have it. I will bring your drinks in moment."

"She seems like a nice waitress" Dan remarked as he watched her leave.

"Dan, you say that about any women who says May I" whispered Mary as she giggled.

"Really?" Dan smiled. "I guess you would know."

"Have you heard from Pat or John?" asked Mary changing the topic.

"No." Dan folded he hands on the table. "Have you?"

"No. But I guess we will be talking to them tomorrow."

Soon the waitress returned with their drinks and left. Once again Dan was watching the waitress as she left. "Dan are you possessed?"

"NO!" He laughed. "I just wanted to tease you!"

Soon their meals were delivered. "Okay Dan. Can we talk work now?" Mary began to chewing her grilled cheese.

"Okay. You know this case is a real mystery. So many unknowns about the known." Dan replied as he crunched into his burger and began to nibble at his fries.

"Yes, that is so true."

They began to share much of the same information that Mary had seen. Dan did not see anything different from her. "So I guess we are on the same page?" Dan asked.

"Yep. We need to know more about Henry Ford from Ohio."

Chapter Seven: Getting to know you

The next day Mary and John met with John and Pat in the briefing room with Steve Williams their boss as they shared information.

"Well you all have found some interesting facts." Williams remarked as he rose and began creating a time line and connection map on the bulletin board. The victims, suspects and places of crime were posted with pictures of them along with other facts. "It is the names which seem so odd. Joe Doe and Henry Ford." He then gave a chuckle, "but no matter how weird, we need to find some more information. Pat and John I want you to visit where Henry Ford lived and see what he did for a living, his friends, associates etcetera and get more information. Dan and Mary go to the crime scene of the murder and see if you find anything."

With chores given, they all left the meeting and began their missions.

"I am a bit sorry we did not get the Henry Ford investigation." Mary said as she and Dan entered the company vehicle to drive to the cabin in the woods.

"Me too. But I am glad we do not have to drive the 300 miles to do our work."

"Yes, Dan that is true. But I kind of wanted to visit my hometown."

"You are from Ohio?"

"Yes, I grew up there but moved away when I joined the FBI."

"What about you Dan. Where are you from?"

39

"I grew up in Pennsylvania, near Pittsburgh."

"So we both came from probably similar backgrounds." Mary remarked as she viewed the trees along the road leading toward the cabin where Henry Ford was killed.

"Yes, I guess we did." He then slowed down, "just how far along this road do we have to go?"

"Another 100 miles. Why don't we listen to some music as we drive?"

"Good Idea"

They continued to learn about one another as they drove. Although they worked in the same office for two years this case is the first one they have been assigned together. Dan was raised on a small farm outside of Pittsburgh while Mary lived in a small city surrounded by mountains, woods, and near the Ohio River. They shared the country atmosphere but Mary was a bit more city oriented.

It took a while, but they finally arrived at the cabin assigned. They had called the owner and planned to meet him there at noon. The sun was shining as they pulled into the parking space near the cabin.

"This is nice. Quiet. Hay look," Dan said as he pointed to the lake in front of the cabin. "I guess Ford planned to fish here."

"He might have. I see a row boat over there." Mary unbuckled her seatbelt and opened her door. Dan followed as they walked toward the cabin. There was a man sitting on the porch.

"Hello! Are you the FBI?" the man asked as he arose from the steps.

"Yes, we are. And you are?"

"I am Forest Green. The owner. I sure hope you guys get this resolved soon. I have been wanting to open this up but due to the crime I have not been allowed."

"Hopefully our investigation will get to the point we can do that. Can we see the crime scene?"

They followed Mr. Green into the room where the body was found and began to search for anything that might have been missed. The axe as well as other clues were in the locked room back at their office building. As they checked, however, they could find no new clues in this room.

"Let's check the outside as well." Mary said as she left the cabin and began to search around the outside rim of the house. Dan followed and looked as well. They then went down to the lake where the boat was. As they checked the boat, they did see some empty wrapping of snacks in the boat. No idea how long they were there but they collected them for evidence.

Soon they thanked Mr. Green and began their trip back to the office.

Chapter Eight: Deeper

The next day Mary drove to work as normal. She was feeling rather tired and confused as she parked her car in the lot and walked into the building. "Hello!" came from behind her as she climbed the stairs which caught her by surprise and she stumbled. Fortunately she was holding on the rail which kept her from falling.

"Careful! Are you alright?" Dan asked as he rushed to her aid. "I did not mean to scare you."

"Dan, it is not your fault my mind was elsewhere."

Dan grabbed her arm and began to lead Mary toward the upcoming door. "I guess I need to make more noise when I enter so as not to take you off guard."

Mary smiled and looked into Dan's eyes. "Yes, I guess you do."

Dan opened the door allowing Mary to enter first. They made their way to the office where their day began.

Soon Pat and John arrived as well and the four of them gathered in small private room to share and discuss what they each have found.

"When we went to Ohio to investigate Henry Ford, we found that he attended college locally. He worked for the police department and retired a few months before his death." Pat explained.

"He never married. He was very private with his personal life. He sure had the talent to hide a crime scene since he was an investigator. I wonder if he was hiding something." John added.

"He did not look of retirement age." Mary noted.

"No, he was only 45 when he retired from there. Quite young but he injured himself on the job and got some compensation." Pat remarked. "I think he also had a large amount of money in investments and had bought himself an annuity quite young."

"So he came to Maryland to vacation after retirement?" Dan asked.

"Looks that way." John quipped.

"The murder site is now being released so the owner of the cabin can re-rent it." Mary added. "But we did get a look at the place and gathered anything that might be a clue. I did find some snack wraps in a boat there but, since it was outside, it might not have anything to do to with the murder. Kids could have used the boat after the murder from adjoining cabins in the area."

"As far as the gas station is concerned, there is no proof or link that what was stolen, I mean the hatchet, was the same type as one found on the bed at the scene but no evidence it is the same one stolen. So we might as well remove it from our investigation." Dan sighed as he announced this fact.

"So, so far, the car may or may not be included in the murder." Mary replied. "There were candy wrappers in the car and snack wraps in the boat but that could probably be a coincidence. But the car was stolen and came from Ohio. So I think the car needs to stay for now."

"Agreed." John said followed by Pat and Dan.

They left the room and Mary submitted their findings to their boss.

Chapter Nine: Reviewing the facts

The next morning Mary awoke with another headache. She had been having them more often these past few weeks. But as the day would progress the aches would diminish. If this would continue, she planned to make an appointment with her doctor but for now with the investigation Mary chose to postpone anything that might interfere.

Once at the office Mary began her normal work day. Soon Steve Williams, their boss, announced a meeting in his office. Pat, Joe. Dan and Mary left their desks with notebooks and pens in hand and entered his office. "Please close the door." Williams said as he pointed toward them. Dan was last to enter and quickly shut the door. "Have a seat." In front of them was a poster board with all the facts. "I have created a board for us to post our evidence which I hope will give us some ideas and clarity over this case."

Williams stood in front of the board and pointed to each fact as he spoke. "According to the original report, the victim was found decapitated with a hatchet at a cabin in Maryland." Then there was a pause. "But I visited the mortuary and he was not decapitated. He was killed with a two blade hatchet but the attack was on the leg which cut his femoral artery and he bled out." Everyone gasped at this revolution. "Which means our killer was weaker than expected or this might be an accident." He then pointed to the board. "After some discussion with the owner of the cabin he told me the axe belonged to the cabin. He gives each cabin an axe which is placed near the fireplace. He has firewood outside the cabin which the renter must bring in, if they want to use it. The cabins have electric heaters so the fireplace is a choice." Then Williams paused. "When the owner found the body, it was in the bedroom but there was wood brought into

49

cabin near the fireplace. But the wood was not stacked but strewn on the floor. Which means the victim could have tripped over the wood and fell on the axe. His cellphone was in the bedroom and to get help he would have had to rush to the bedroom. He was wearing heavy pants so the blood soaked much of it up and he could have tried to keep the blade on the wound to slow the bleeding, which could explain the lack of blood droplets until the bedroom."

"Isn't that a bit farfetched?" asked Joe. "How could he have had the strength to hold it in his leg as he went to the bedroom? Also that vein would have caused him to bleed out in 2-5 minutes."

"What about how he got there? Who was it that paid for the cabin with bad check? John Smith does not exist." remarked Pat.

"Who is the John Doe who owned the car? For what purpose is the hidden identity?" Dan questioned as he scratched his head.

"Could have John Smith, the cabin renter, and John Doe, the car owner, been the victim? Could Henry Ford, the retired cop, be them? If so, why would he want to hide his identity? Why was he really here in Maryland?" Mary questioned.

"All good questions. Perhaps this is more complex than we anticipated. I think we need to know more about the victim, especially if he was single and his private life was so private. I would like all of you to look more into his past."

Chapter 10: Researching begins

This time Mary and Dan were sent to Ohio where Henry Ford worked and lived. They were to interview people who might have known him. Williams thought that since Mary and Dan grew up near that area, that perhaps they would be the best to investigate there.

Joe and Pat were to assist Williams with the local area and see if anything points to why Henry Ford came to Maryland besides a vacation.

Once Mary and Dan neared the Ohio Valley area they chose to check into the motel the main office had booked for them for the next three weeks.

"Look there is a parking spot on the left." Mary said as her motioned Dan toward the area.

Dan smiled and slowly drove into the spot Mary seemed adamant to use. "You're kind a picky aren't you?" He laughed as he braked and turn of the ignition putting it in park.

"I'm not picky!" she quipped laughing as well. "I just thought I might be useful."

Laughing they both unbuckled their seat belts and left the vehicle. "What time to we have to be at the police station?' she asked.

"Not until 2 PM. So we have time to register, get to our rooms and eat lunch." Dan replied as he opened the trunk lifting the luggage onto the asphalt. "Boy you bag is really heavy! Glad it is on wheels!" He teased handing the luggage handle over to Mary.

"I call it my weight lifting luggage. To help me keep fit." She said teasing him right back.

Dan closed the truck and followed Mary both dragging their wheeled bags behind them. Once reaching the door, Dan, as usual, held the door for Mary and let her enter first. The sign in desk was just ahead where a young man was waiting for them. "Good morning. How are you today?" he asked.

"We are fine. You should have reservations for Dan Jones and Mary Fife. We are to be here for three weeks." Dan responded.

The clerk checked his log. "Yes, you have an adjoining rooms 218 and 219" Mary and Dan looked at one another and back at the clerk. "Your office requested that so you could do your work without disruption of the other guests." He clerk looked at Dan "Are you signing for both rooms?"

"Yes, I can do that." Dan quickly took the pen from the clerk's hand and signed them both in.

"Here are your keys." Two room keys were handed to Dan. "Have a nice stay and if you have any questions or issues please let me know." He then pointed to the elevator. "You may use the elevator or the stairs next to them."

"Thank you." Dan replied. "Mary, you may choose which room you want once we get there."

They entered the elevator and Dan pushed the second floor button. Soon the doors closed and they rose to their floor.

There was a weird silence until the elevator stopped and the doors opened. "This is strange. Adjoining rooms." Mary whispered.

"Yes it is. But I guess it means we can communicate and work together better." Dan whispered back.

Then they both laughed as they reached there adjoining rooms. "Okay. Let's try 218 first." Dan then opened the door and they entered the room. It was a nice room with queen sized bed in the middle. It had a TV, phone, desk, and closet with a bathroom. Off to the right was a door with a latch. Dan lowered the latch and opened the door. There was another door on the other side but no handle to open it. The back of the opened door was the same. "I guess they made it that way so they could rent them out separately and keep privacy." Mary responded. "Guess I need to see 219. I will go an open that door and meet you here." Mary left but did not take her luggage. Soon the other door opened and Mary was grinning at Dan. "So unless we need joint communications we still have our privacy." Dan returned her smile. "I guess so." He then entered her room to find it much like his. "You want which room?" he asked. "I think I keep this one" she responded.

"So lunch in a half hour?" he asked as he began to shut his adjoining door.

"Yes. Knock on the door when you're ready." Mary smiled and shut her door.

Chapter 11: Lunch and the Station

Within about 20 minutes Dan knocked on the adjoining room door. Mary opened her side smiling as she spoke. "Yes, I am ready for lunch. Fast food good enough so we can make sure we are on time?"

Dan returned her smile. "Sounds good. Meet you outside."

They closed their adjoining doors and met in hallway joking as they made their way to main desk where they asked the staff where the nearest fast food was located and how far away the police station was. After gathering that information they left the motel.

The sun was shining and it was getting warmer as they reached the restaurant. After ordering their sandwiches they found a seats where there was a large window. Fortunately, across the street was the police station.

"I am so glad everything is close. I did not want to drive. Our 6 hour trip was enough for today." Dan remarked as they sat down.

"I agree. The drive was long." Mary began to eat her lunch.

"What is our game plan?" Dan asked just before he also began munching on his burger and fries.

"I thought we would interview the staff who knew him and then look at some of the cases he worked on."

"Mary, I would also like to visit his old neighborhood and see if anyone remembers him."

"I think that is a good idea. Getting some clues on his personal life might give us a lead."

Soon they finished their meal and crossed the street to the station. It was rather large building which housed not just the police but city workers such as mayor, clerks, medical files, and property files. There was a sign with an arrow that pointed to the police station which they followed and reached a greeting area.

Dan walked to the greeter. "Hello. We have a meeting with the captain. Dan Jones and Mary Fife from the FBI."

"Oh, yes, I was made aware of your appointment. The captain will be right with you." The clerk replied as she spoke into a box to let the captain be made aware of their arrival.

The captain left his office and made his way to Dan and Mary. The captain offered his hand as he spoke, "Hello, I am Captain Joseph Hess. How may we be of assistance?"

They should hands and introduced themselves and then walked into the captain's office. "Have a seat" the captain said as he sat in his chair behind his desk.

Mary and Dan sat I front of his desk. "Thank you for taking the time to speak with us. We are working on the possible murder case of your past officer Henry Ford. He was found in a cabin in Maryland. We need some information to determine if this was a murder or accident."

"Yes, we were sorry to hear of his demise. He was a private man but a good cop."

"Did he have any close friends here at the precinct?" Mary asked.

"No. Like I said he was private. Did not share his life."

"Didn't that concern you?" Dan asked.

"Why? As long as he did his job that was enough."

"He retired due to job injury. What was the incident?" Dan responded.

"He was trying to save a neighbor of his from falling. He climbed to the roof to help but slipped and fell. The neighbor died."

"Why was the neighbor on the roof?" Mary questioned.

"We don't know. Other than Henry, no other witnesses were found."

"Who died?" Dan asked.

"Her name was Diane Webb."

"Does she have any relatives we can talk with?" Dan asked as he kept writing notes.

"Not sure. I can give you the case file. It may tell you more."

"Great. We would like to also see other case files he worked on to try and understand a bit about him and his work"

"Sure I will have my staff made aware. You can use one of our private rooms as well to view them."

Soon their conversation ended and Mary and Dan were lead to a private room where they waited for the files.

While they sat around a large table they noticed a camera in the room. Dan and Mary moved close together. Dan whispered to Mary, "We are being watched. Are they hiding something?"

Whispering back Mary responded, "I noticed as well. Good question. I think we need to keep whispering while in here." Dan nodded.

Soon the staff arrived with the Diane Webb file and a few others.

"Surely he worked on more cases than these" Dan addressed the staffer.

"Yes, but these are the most recent. It will take longer for other files."

"Fine. But we need to go back to the beginning when he was hired. We plan to be here three weeks. So I expect to have all the files available the next two days. Also we want the camera removed. Our investigation needs to be private and this room needs to be locked by us so we need a key. No one can handle the files once we have them."

"Yes, sir. I will get you a key and relay the requests to the captain."

Chapter 12: The Investigation Begins

Over the next two days Mary and Dan gathered several files that shared some information that might be relevant to their investigation. They made copies of those files to take with them to review and keep them as evidence.

On third day, they drove to the neighborhood where Diane Webb died and Henry Ford tried to save her.

Dan parked their car and they quickly began to knock on doors next door to where Diane lived.

They began with the next door neighbors of the event who might have known Diane Webb. The crime scene house was now occupied by a new owner. As they approached, the female occupant of the past crime scene came onto their porch. "Hello." Dan said as he chose to greet them. "We are with the FBI and are investigating the accident of the prior owner of your home. So to bother you, but I was wondering if you knew Diane Webb?"

"No. I did not know her. I was just told she committed suicide by jumping off the roof." She looked quite a bit surprised. "Why are you investigating?"

"The officer who attempted to save her has suspiciously died recently." Dan replied as he and Mary stopped at the property gate.

"Sorry to hear that. I am afraid I have no information to share. Good luck with your investigation." The resident then sat on the porch swing and opened her newspaper and began reading.

Dan and Mary looked at one another and approached another next door neighbor's home. They knocked on the door began waiting for an answer. Soon a gentleman answered the door. "Hello. I am Dan Jones and this is Mary Fife. We are with the FBI and investigating the death of Diane Webb. Are you the resident of this home and did you know her?" asked Dan.

"Yes, I live here and knew her." He looked a bit uneasy. "Why are you investigating her suicide?"

"Recently, the officer who attempted to save her suspiciously died and we are looking at possible reasons and suspects. Did you witness the death?"

"No. I was not home. But that officer knew her and visited her often. They were dating. He spent a lot of time here."

"How was their relationship?"

"They were dating so I guess it was good. I did not spend much time talking to either of them. They kept to themselves."

The conversation continued but no major information other than the dating was discovered. As they interviewed the other neighbors the story seemed to be the same.

Dan and Mary finished and entered their car. "Mary any thoughts?" Dan asked as he prepared to leave.

"Dan, Henry knew her. They all agreed on that. But no one really knew either of them. Including Henry's other officers and staff. The department apparently did not know he was dating her or, if they did know, they failed to enter it into the files."

"I am surprised that fact did not show up. Either they knew and were hiding it or they never were made aware of it when they investigated or they did not feel it important." Dan replied.

"Yes, weird." Mary pondered. "Were they protecting him or themselves?"

"Or were they that incompetent." Dan mused.

Chapter 13: The Weekend Trip

It was dark. The moon was full and glowed creating shadows resembling those created in daylight with the sun. Cicadas sounding their voices were heard among the silence while lightening bugs added sparkle within the trees and brush. A large shadow began to emerge and roam the woods. It began walking slowly, pausing on occasion then walking once again. The brush was heard moving as the shadow continued to make its way toward a cabin in the distance. It was then I realized the shadow was me. But what was I doing in the forest?

Slowly I moved closer to the cabin entrance and began to open the door. It creaked slowly as it opened. I was curious but afraid. The cabin was empty. A fireplace was seen across the room. As I slowly entered my footsteps echoed. Why was I here?

A wolf's howl began. It was getter louder. The wolf was coming. I quickly closed the door and grabbed an abandoned chair the came into view from behind the door. Placing the chair against the door, I braced for the possible attack to come.

Suddenly Mary awoke. She was breaking out in cold sweat and felt startled by the dream. "Why am I having this same dream?" Then slowly she got out of bed and noticed it was almost time to get up so she turned off her alarm. This dream has been bothering her for weeks. It was quite a puzzle.

Today Dan and Mary planned to go for the weekend to his parent's farm to relax for a few days. It has been a busy week and as well, they both felt they needed a break.

Soon Dan came knocking on the door. "Mary are you ready to go?" Mary opened the door with her luggage rolling behind her. "Yep I am ready. I really need this mini-vacation."

Laughing Dan waited while Mary locked her door and then they both left rolling their luggage with them. They had advised the clerk they were still keeping their rooms but making a brief weekend trip the prior day. So they had made sure their rooms would be still theirs when they returned.

Once they and their luggage was inside the car they began their trek. Dan's parents lived outside Pittsburgh Pennsylvania on a small farm. The trip was about one hour away from their motel so not too much of a drive. The sun was shining and they enjoyed the scenery along the way. They made a pact that they would not discuss work so they could really relax.

Once off the busy highway they were surrounded with grasslands, woods and nature. That alone made them more relaxed. "How much further?" Mary asked feeling excited to see where Dan grew up.

"We are almost there. See the farm just ahead?" Mary nodded. "That is our destination." Dan grinned as he slowed down and turned right into the small paved road which lead to the farm house.

They exited the vehicle and felt the warm breeze. The birds were chirping in the nearby trees which were waving gently. "What beautiful place!" Mary remarked as she followed Dan toward the house each towing their luggage.

"Yes, I miss it." Dan replied as he opened the door to let Mary in ahead of him. Once inside Mary was stunned by the comfortable atmosphere.

"Son! Missed you!" Dan's father entered the hallway and reached to hug his son.

"I've missed you as well." Dan said as he hugged his dad as well. "Where is mom?"

Then a women entered. "Son! I've missed you so much!" She hugged Dan as well. "And who is this lovely lady?"

"Mom, Dad, this is my co-worker Mary Fife. We are working on a case about an hour away and thought we'd come visit for the weekend."

"Nice you meet you my dear." Dan's mom and dad said as they shook her hand. "Well let's get you two setup for the stay. We have a guest room for you Mary and Dan can use his old room."

"I can take her to the guest room." Dan said as he moved toward the stairs. "Follow me."

Soon Mary found herself in a small but comfortable room with a view of the grassy fields and forest. She felt comfortable and was so glad to have come.

As the day progressed, Mary got to know more about Dan via his parents. Stories of childhood and growing up were shared. Dan was very helpful as a child and loved the forest. He was not into hunting but did love the wildlife.

Then Mary was asked to share her life. "I really do not remember much about my childhood. We lived in the small city but my I never knew my dad. Mom dated the man next door but I really do not remember much about him."

"I am sorry you did not know you father." Dan's mom remarked.

"I wish I could remember more but my memories are more about my college life and working with the FBI.

Chapter 14: The Case

Mary and Dan collected more data and facts as the days and weeks passed. Every week end they would visit Dan's parents and developed a closer friendship. Mary was feeling like she was finding a family once again. She lost her mom while she was in college and had no knowledge of any other relatives. But she was happier now than she had been in the past.

"Mary are you okay?"

Mary opened her eyes and found herself at their normal DC area office sitting across from Dan. "I'm fine. I did not get much sleep last night. Have had a headache."

"Did you take some aspirin?"

"Yes. But it has not worked yet."

Just then the speaker turned on. "Briefing room for Henry Ford Case in 15."

"Looking forward to how they analyzed the data." Dan quipped as he arose. "You need help getting up?"

Mary was a bit off balanced as she gradually stood. "I'm okay. Thanks for caring." She gave Dan a quick smile as he waved her forward and followed her to the large briefing room.

They sat and watched as other investigators entered and finally the lead Steve Williams reached the podium. The microphone squeaked before he spoke. "Thanks to all of your efforts we now have enough facts to render a conclusion."

There was a large screen behind him that lit up as the lights in the room dimmed. Williams was at the podium with a light over his notes as he read.

"Henry Ford was a policeman and recently retired due to injuries sustained when trying to save a woman from jumping of her roof."

He paused. "But the investigation by the local police forgot to note that he was not only a neighbor of the jumping woman but he was dating her. When the local department realized he did not give that information, they chose to hide it to protect their image in the community. They required Henry to retire early or face charges of withholding information or more."

The room became very quiet. "But by making this pact, they also withheld vital information and are awaiting charges. Attorneys are working on this going forward."

Dan smiled. Williams continued. "But there is much more. We suspect that Henry Ford may have killed the woman. According to neighbors, Henry could be verbally and physically abusive to the woman he supposedly saved."

Williams began story telling. "We believe that Henry was worried that he would be charged with murder in the future. So he began a plot to disappear. He left his town with a new identity and chose to keep hiding by keeping far from cities. Thus he rented a cabin, got rid of the car he used which he created a fate auto ID to create an even deeper hide."

On the screen was being shown the evidence as he was talking. Including the cabin pictures.

"Once at the cabin he began to hunker down. Part of that process was using chopped wood for the fireplace."

Williams's picture of the fireplace area was shown on the screen. He then use his laser pen to point to items.

"This is the crime scene. Notice how the logs are strewn in front of the fireplace. Henry's injuries from the fall of the roof made him off kilter when walking. It would have been difficult for him to maneuver the logs, especially get them into the fireplace without falling. Our vison is that he attempted to lift the logs and kept dropping them and they rolled. While attempting to recover the logs, he fell. Only this time his fall thrust him onto the axe or hatchet which was sitting blade up within the area of his fall."

The bedroom in the cabin was shown with Henry's body on the bed.

"Once he realized he had a serious wound, he knew in order to stay alive he needed to keep the hatchet in the wound to avoid bleeding out. Thus we did not see blood until the bedroom when he could no longer hold it in place."

Williams pointed to the bed. "Notice. He was wearing heavy pants which could have easily held the blood until he reached the bedroom. The way the wound is located he would have hit a vein or artery which could bleed quickly within minutes. It takes less than one minute to reach the bedroom from where the accident occurred. At the most two to three minutes for him. He went to bedroom because that is where his cellphone was and he needed to call 911. Reaching for the cell meant releasing the axe. That action caused the bleeding to increase and he then passed out. That passing out led him to bleed to death quickly."

Williams then paused. "Our department has ruled his death to be an accident. But that does not mean he is not guilty of murder, and brutality to the woman he supposedly saved."

Williams paused again. "In some respects perhaps fate or God gave judgement where our justice system failed."

The Briefing Room was full of chatter after the reveal. Williams then remarked. "Thank you for your time. Please return to your duties."

Dan was smiling as he stood and moved to leave. Mary stood but once again felt woozy. "Dan, I don't feel right. Can you give me a hand?"

Dan concerned grabbed her hand but as soon as she began leaving the room she collapsed and fell on the floor. Dan was frantic as he watched her begin jerking and yelled, "Help! Call 911 get an ambulance! She is having secures!"

Chapter 15: The Cabin

It was dark. The moon was full and glowed creating shadows resembling those created in daylight with the sun. Cicadas sounding their voices were heard among the silence while lightening bugs added sparkle within the trees and brush. A large shadow began to emerge and roam the woods. It began walking slowly, pausing on occasion then walking once again. The brush was heard moving as the shadow continued to make its way toward a cabin in the distance. It was then I realized the shadow was me. But what was I doing in the forest?

Slowly I moved closer to the cabin entrance and began to open the door. It creaked slowly as it opened. I was curious but afraid. The cabin was empty. A fireplace was seen across the room. As I slowly entered my footsteps echoed. Why was I here?

A wolf's howl began. It was getter louder. The wolf was coming. I quickly closed the door and grabbed an abandoned chair the came into view from behind the door. Placing the chair against the door, I braced for the possible attack to come.

This time she turned and the fireplace was lit. The room looked like the crime scene from Henry Ford. "What the F....!" She screamed as she was touched from behind. She jumped and ran to the other side of the room. The howling had stopped, the chair was no longer blocking the door. Fear rose inside her as she glanced about the room searching for what touched her.

Then a shadow appeared before her. But shadow looked just like her. "What is this? What kind of freaking joke is this?"

The shadow smiled. "Hello Mary. Let me introduce myself."

Mary's eyes widened. Fear was very present on her face."

"I'm your wall. By wall I mean, I am another version of you. I have hid myself from you to protect you."

"Protect me from what?" Mary asked as she grabbed a poker from the wall.

"From everything." The shadow grinned a rather evil grin. "I've been protecting you from Henry for years."

"Your nuts! I never met him until he died."

"True, but only because I took over."

"Took over what?

"Why, your body of course."

Mary began to shake. "What are you? The devil?"

"No. I am your, let's say double." The shadow smiled. "I was created actually by you when Henry first hit you and molested you. He hurt your mom first but I hid that from you as well. He was mean and evil. So you created me so that you could cope. You are so weak. It was me that killed Henry. When your mom died he hunted you down. He needed either your mom or you to bully. He wanted to pick up where you were before you went off to college. He molested and beat you until you left. When his "new" neighbor rebelled he killed her. Now he wanted to get you back. He hid his identy to protect himself but to also make it easier to find you and get you back. When he called you I took over. I agreed to meet him at this cabin. He smiled and went to bedroom to "wait" for you. I grabbed the axe and hit him in the leg so make him bleed to death. Then I made the room look like an accident."

"I am not weak! I am strong and I would not willingly let anyone beat or molest me."

84

"Which is why, I was created. But I am tired of protecting you. I have lived your bad life and now I want to live yours. I want you to release me to be you."

"No way. I do not know you and I do not trust you." Mary began to arm herself.

"Okay. Then I will take it." The shadow grabbed the axe. "Poker vs axe. I think I have the upper hand!"

Mary suddenly felt anger she never felt before. It felt powerful but also made her fearful. She blocked the axe from hitting her with her poker. They struggled and both pulled back and dropped their weapons. They began to lunge at one another grabbing throats, biting and kicking.

"Give me the good life, Mary!"

"Never" Mary yelled.

Then all went black.

Chapter 16: The Awaking

Dan was in the waiting room as the doctors were evaluating Mary. He was a bit nervous that she might be leaving this life soon.

"Dan, thank you for sharing the health and some history about Mary" The doctor said as he entered. "The X-rays have shown a blood clot, created, perhaps, from childhood, is being removed as we speak. The clot could explain her headaches, secure, and loss of memory from childhood."

"Thank you for helping her. Please keep me aware of progress."

Hours later, Dan was sitting next to Mary as she lay in bed. He was hopeful that she would recover.

Mary felt groggy and heard machines around her as she opened her eyes.

The nurse rushed in because of the noises on the machine waking Dan who had nodded off. "What's happening?" He asked.

"Good news. She is awake and seems to be doing well."

Dan smiled and held Mary's hand. Mary's eyes locked onto Dan's and she spoke. "Where am I?"

"You're in the hospital. You had a secure as we left the briefing room."

"A secure?" she asked

"Yes. You had a blood clot, possibly from childhood, and it was removed. It explains your memory loss, headaches, as well. You will be alright now."

"Thank you for saving me."

After a few days Mary was allowed to be released from the hospital but Dan insisted to stay at her home to take care of her. Their work agreed to let Dan work from Mary's home as he helped her recover.

During this time they became more aware that they were in love with one another and discussed with their employer if they could still work together. Fortunately their boss was happy for them and supported them.

They eloped and began working once again as before.

"Mary? Are you okay?" Dan asked as she was staring out the window of their office.

"Yes. I am fine. Stop worrying so much. The "problem" is gone and I feel much better."

Mary never mentioned her dream about the shadow and would feel a bit guilty that Henry was killed-- if the shadow was real. But she would not have been the one who controlled it. The shadow is gone. They may have shared the same body but no more. Her body, however, if the shadow was real, would be both guilty and innocent.

About the Author

Donna Sako was raised in Wheeling, West Virginia and currently living in Taneytown, Maryland. She earned her Bachelor of Arts Board of regents Degree in 1976 from West Liberty State College which is now West Liberty University. Her studies included Social Science Comprehensive, Home Economics and Law. In 2001 she retired from Verizon Communications. She owned and operated Alpha Research, Inc. and served as Executive Director of the Taneytown Chamber of Commerce. During her working career she also served as a Customer Service Representative, Small Business Counselor, Consultant, Teacher, and Competitive Intelligence Specialist.

www.ingramcontent.com/pod-product-compliance
Lightning Source LLC
Chambersburg PA
CBHW020635130626
46552CB00003B/1245